Building

of Carnegie
Center of Brazos Valley History

Bryan Firefighters, 1928.
John Stasny is the driver of the truck
on the left, a 1921 Stutz.
Photo courtesy of Carnegie Center of Brazos Valley History

The FIREGATOR

Written by Debbie Leland   Illustrated by Ann Hollis Rife

Wildflower Run Publishing

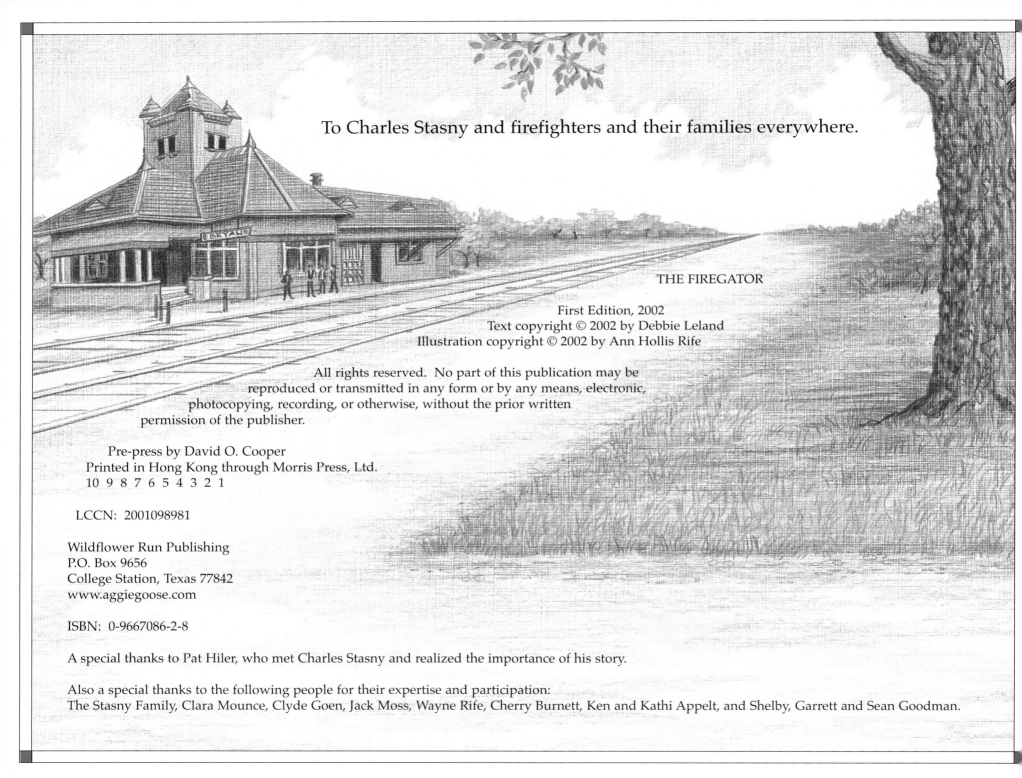

To Charles Stasny and firefighters and their families everywhere.

THE FIREGATOR

First Edition, 2002
Text copyright © 2002 by Debbie Leland
Illustration copyright © 2002 by Ann Hollis Rife

Pre-press by David O. Cooper
Printed in Hong Kong through Morris Press, Ltd.
10 9 8 7 6 5 4 3 2 1

LCCN: 2001098981

Wildflower Run Publishing
P.O. Box 9656
College Station, Texas 77842
www.aggiegoose.com

ISBN: 0-9667086-2-8

A special thanks to Pat Hiler, who met Charles Stasny and realized the importance of his story.

Also a special thanks to the following people for their expertise and participation:
The Stasny Family, Clara Mounce, Clyde Goen, Jack Moss, Wayne Rife, Cherry Burnett, Ken and Kathi Appelt, and Shelby, Garrett and Sean Goodman.

ZIP, ZIP, ZING, the tops were spinning fast. They twirled in circles like rainbows on a merry-go-round. *ZAP!* Charles's top veered left toward the depot, and stopped just underneath the rose bushes.

"Rats," said Charles reaching inside the bushes.

But he didn't feel his wooden top, he felt something long and leathery instead. *SWISH, SWISH, SWISH,* something moved inside the bushes.

Charles jumped back. *BLINK, BLINK, BLINK,* he could
hardly believe his eyes. Right there, in front of him, sat a bonafied
alligator with big alligator eyes, an alligator snout, and a long
alligator tail. The other boys grabbed their tops and ran. But not Charles,
he noticed how the alligator gently cradled the top in his mouth. *WHAP, WHAP, WHAP,*
the alligator wagged his tail as if he were a friendly puppy. This was no ordinary alligator!

TIP, *TAP*, *TAP*, the alligator followed Charles home. Since Charles's papa was a firefighter for Bryan, Texas, his family lived in the basement of the new Municipal Building, which also served as the fire station.

"Can I keep him?" Charles begged.

The alligator begged, too.

"I'm sorry," said Papa, "but the fire station is no place for a gator."

Charles and the gator hung their heads and walked away.

"Come on," said Charles. "Let's go downtown."

As they walked by the Palace Theater, *SNIFF*, *SNIFF*, *SNIFF* went the gator's nose. What was that smell? Popcorn! Everywhere! *SNAP*, *SNAP*, *SNAP*, every kernel of popcorn was *GONE*, *GONE*, *GONE*, popcorn bags and all.

"The theater is no place for a gator," said Mr. Schulman shaking his head.

TIP, *TAP*, *TAP*, they walked across the street to the Carnegie Library. *WHAP*, *WHAP*, *WHAP*, went the gator's tail, and *SWOOSH*, *SWOOSH*, *SWOOSH*, pages flipped and flapped, and books flew everywhere.

"The library is no place for a gator," said Miss Rogers pointing them out the door.

"Downtown is no place for a gator," said Constable Conlee. "That gator has gotta go."

"Come on," said Charles quickly.

At the park, *DOWN, UP, DOWN*, the gator tried to 'walk the dog' with his yo-yo. But before Charles could say "lickety-split," they were both wrapped in yo-yo string like yo-yo mummies.

"Here," said Charles sliding the gator his lucky marble. "Try this."

But it was during the game of marbles, when Momma Cat strolled down the sidewalk with her five kittens, *SWISH, SWISH, SWISH*, all six tails high in the air.

At the pharmacy, Charles and the gator sat down to eat their double decker ice cream cones. *AAHHH, AAHHH, CHOOO*, the gator sneezed at the wrong time. Ice cream flew off the cones, and a cherry landed on the tip of Constable Conlee's nose.

CHARGE! The gator took out after those cats like a posse in pursuit of an outlaw. Marbles scattered everywhere, and Momma Cat and her five kittens scrambled up the live oak tree.

"*MEOW, MEOW, MEOW,*" they cried. Finally, Mr. Jenkins, another firefighter, came to their rescue.

"The park is no place for a gator," said Mr. Jenkins. "That gator has gotta go."

"Let's go to the schoolhouse," said Charles hopefully.

At school the gator sat perfectly straight in his chair. Maybe he could be the teacher's pet. At recess the children chanted, "Red rover, red rover, send gator right over."
BUMPETY, BUMP, BUMP, the gator knocked the whole team over like a set of dominoes, one right after the other.

And if that wasn't bad enough, during leap frog, the gator jumped, BOING, BOING, BOING. But his one-and-over was too far over, and he landed smack dab in the middle of Miss Dearing's lap.

Aesop's
Fables
p. 79-8

Test

Friday

Charles quickly grabbed the gator and led him
to right field. Surely nothing could go wrong in a
simple game of baseball.   But the gator was tired from
his busy day, and he *YAWNED, YAWNED, YAWNED,*
at the wrong time. *OOPS! GULP! UH-OH!*
The gator swallowed the ball. Game over.
"I'm sorry," said Miss Dearing sadly,
"but the schoolhouse is no place for a gator."
Charles and the gator hung their heads down low.
"Come on," said Charles. "Let's go home."

When they arrived at the fire station, Mama said,
"That gator has gotta stay outside."

Charles put some biscuits and milk outside for the gator. He listened to the radio with Mama and Papa for awhile, and then he went to bed. He was feeling lonely and sad. Meanwhile, the gator curled his tail up underneath himself on the front porch. He was feeling lonely and sad. Maybe everyone was right. Maybe this was no place for a gator.

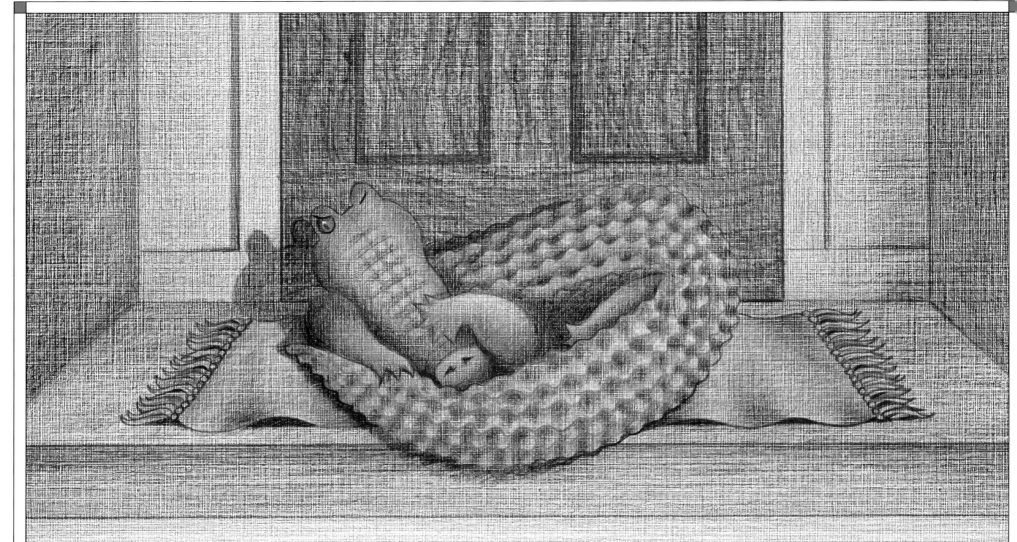

It was nearly midnight and the whole town was asleep when the gator woke up. His skin felt extra crinkly and dry. He put his long snout in the air, *SNIFF*, *SNIFF*, *SNIFF*. What was that smell? *SNIFF*, *SNIFF*, *SNIFF*, again. Oh no! Smoke! Black clouds billowed out of the lumberyard on Main Street.

WHAP, WHAP, WHAP,
the gator hit his tail against the door.
Nothing happened. *WHAP, WHAP, WHAP,*
again, harder this time.
Finally, Charles opened the door, and sleepily asked,
"What is it?"
TAP, TAP, TAP, the gator pointed his tail toward the smoke.
Charles saw the smoke and yelled, "Fire!"

Charles ran to the rope.
The gator ran to the rope.
DOWN, UP, DOWN,
they pulled.
CLING, CLANG, CLING,
the fire bell rang from
the rooftop.
Papa grabbed his boots,
his jacket, and his hat, and
ran to Pumper Truck No 3.
Mama flipped the switch
to the fire alarm.
WHEEE, OOO, WHEEE,
the siren screamed across
the city alerting the
volunteer firefighters.

The fire trucks raced down the narrow streets. The townspeople gathered outside. The firefighters pulled out the hoses. Flames reached for them through the windows. The orange feet of the fire danced in the darkness.

The gator heard a noise. It sounded like crying. He rushed inside the burning building. The firefighters pushed against the heat with water. Fire flew at them like dragons' breath.

Charles held his breath waiting for the gator.

The townspeople held their breath waiting for the gator.

Smoke filled the air until it was so thick they could taste it.

Come on, thought Charles, *you can do it*.

They were just about to give up hope, when Charles shouted, "There he is. I see his snout." *CHARGE!* The gator ran out of the building like the cavalry charges into battle. Flames shot up around him like fireworks on the Fourth of July.

Riding on his back was Momma Cat and her five kittens, *MEOW, MEOW, MEOW*.
Everyone cheered.

The firefighters worked long hours to put the fire out. And the next day there was a celebration at the fire station. That gator was a hero!

"This gator has gotta stay," cried Charles.

And everyone agreed.
The fire station was the perfect place for a firegator.

A Place In Time

In December, 1929, eight-year-old Charles Stasny and his parents moved into the new Municipal Building, which also served as the fire station. At that time Charles's father, John Stasny, was the only paid firefighter for the City of Bryan, Texas. When Charles's friends came to visit him downtown at the fire station, they sometimes went roller skating on the concrete pad down by the train depot, rode bikes, spun tops, and often played marbles.

Charles Stasny school photo.

"The library was right across the street," said Charles, "so I read lots of books." Popular at that time were Hardy Boys adventure stories, jacks and yo-yos. *The Bryan Daily Eagle* reported on July 13, 1929, that Jessie Thomas yo-yoed 2,033 times without a miss or a flip.

"There was always a movie to go see at the Palace, or the Dixie, or the Queen Theater," said Charles. "Used to cost 40 cents to see a movie." Talking pictures came to the Palace Theater in Bryan, Texas in 1929.

"We didn't have 911 back then," said Charles. "When a call came to the fire station, Mother turned on the siren, and then took calls from the volunteers to tell them where the fire was located." Sometimes if the siren didn't work, she would ring the bell on top of the roof. Charles's mother, Jennie Stasny, was of such "slight build" that when she rang the bell, the rope would often pull her feet off the floor. The original fire bell from the rooftop of the Municipal Building is now located outside the Bryan Public Library.

John Stasny drove the 1929 American LaFrance pumper truck. "The streets used to be very narrow," Charles said. "Sometimes, when cars were parked on both sides of the street, the driver had to pick out the oldest car, and roll the fire truck right over it."

For a short time, two alligators actually lived in the window well outside the fire station, though they were soon released to a more natural environment.

Charles and his dog, Spot.

"We didn't have a Dalmatian at the fire station," said Charles. "But I did have a dog, a fox terrier. His name was Spot, and he loved to chase motorcycles."

Charles Stasny lived in the Municipal Building until 1942, when he went to serve in WWII. In 1947, he married Mary Anne. They have three sons, one daughter and eight grandchildren. Charles served as a volunteer fireman for several years.

The Municipal Building, designed by Texas A&M architect, F.E. Geisecke, is now listed in the National Register of Historic Places, and is now the permanent home of the Children's Museum of the Brazos Valley. Where Charles once sat and listened to the Grand Ole Opry on the radio with his parents on Saturday nights, children can now play the piano and make their own music in the "Sounds Around Town" exhibit. Where Mrs. Stasny used to quilt and sew, children can create their own stories on a typewriter in "Brazos News." Where Mr. Stasny and other firemen once sat for hours playing a domino game called "moon," children can pull on a pair of rubber boots and fire pants, put on a fire hat, and become real firefighters. And for that moment, when their imaginations soar, when children can be anything they want to be, time stands still.

Snow firefighter at the fire station

Bryan Firefighters, circa 1926.
John Stasny, top row, 4th from left.
Photo courtesy of Bryan Fire Department.